Flower and Fairy Alphabet
Coloring Book

Darcy May

DOVER PUBLICATIONS, INC.
MINEOLA, NEW YORK

Bibliographical Note

Flower and Fairy Alphabet Coloring Book is a new work, first published by Dover Publications, Inc., in 1996.

International Standard Book Number: 0-486-29024-7

Manufactured in the United States of America
Dover Publications, Inc., 31 East 2nd Street, Mineola, N.Y. 11501

NOTE

People know and love flowers, which add so much beauty to our lives. But not everyone knows that there are special fairies associated with each flower. Darcy May has captured the likenesses of 26 of these flowers—one for each letter of the alphabet—with the appropriate fairies. All they need is the application of crayon, magic marker, colored pencil or watercolor to bring out their loveliness.

Azalea Fairy

Bluebell Fairy

Columbine Fairy

Daisy Fairy

Edelweiss Fairy

Foxglove Fairy

Gladiolus Fairy

Honeysuckle Fairy

Iris Fairy

Jonquil Fairy

K

Knapweed Fairy

Lilac Fairy

Morning Glory Fairy

Nasturtium Fairy

Oleander Fairy

Pansy Fairies

Queen Anne's Lace Fairy

R

Rose Fairies

Unicorn Plant Flower Fairy

Violet Fairy

Wisteria Fairy

Xeranthemum Fairy

Yarrow Fairy

Zinnia Fairy